GIGGLING GERTIE

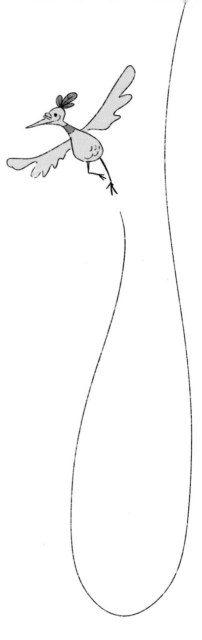

**FIVE
MILE**

Five Mile, an imprint of
Bonnier Publishing Australia
Level 6, 534 Church Street
Richmond, Victoria 3121
www.fivemile.com.au

This is a *Sally Rippin* PRESENTS book.

First published 2017
Text copyright © Sally Rippin and Fiona Harris, 2017
Artwork copyright © Scott Edgar, 2017
Design by Kristy Lund-White
All rights reserved
Cataloguing-in-Publication data is available from
the National Library of Australia

Printed in China 5 4 3 2 1

Sally Rippin PRESENTS...

SUPER MOOPERS

GIGGLING GERTIE

WORDS BY FIONA HARRIS

ART BY SCOTT EDGAR

FIVE MILE

Welcome to MOOPERTOWN!

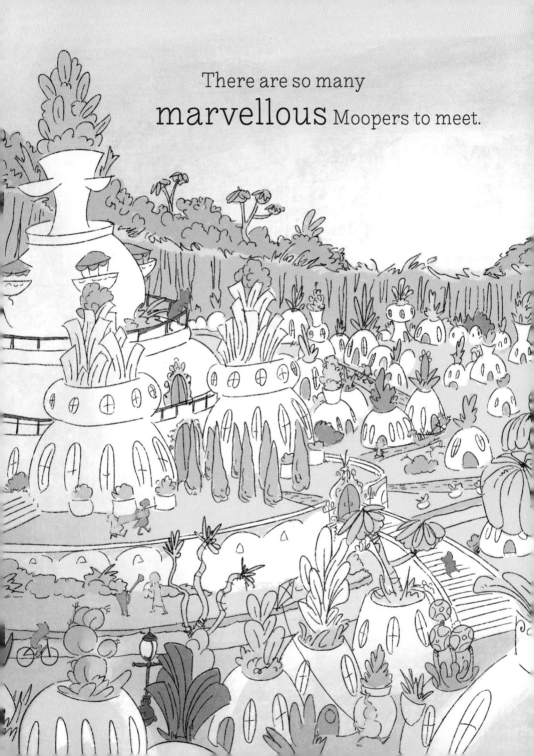

There are so many **marvellous** Moopers to meet.

Let's take a look!

Who's that on the
Town Hall steps?

Oh. I hear **giggling**.
Can you guess who that might be?

It's
Giggling
Gertie!

Gertie giggles at EVERYTHING.

She giggles in sad movies.

She giggles in serious plays.

She even giggles in fancy restaurants.

Which can sometimes be very messy indeed!

Gertie! Not *everything* is funny!

Today, Lord Hoity Toity Baron von Mooper will be arriving for his annual tour of Moopertown.

Everyone is taking this

very
seriously.

Except Gertie, it seems.

Gertie works for Mayor Beadle. She has a **very important** list of **very important** things that need to be ticked off for their **very important** visitor.

'How are the decorations coming along?'

Gertie asks Margaret.

'I'm worried I won't get everything done in time!' Margaret moans.

Just then, a gust of wind sweeps up the banner.

It flies into the air, and drops right on to Harry's head.

Gertie **giggles.**

Margaret scowls.

'It's **NOT FUNNY,** Gertie!'

'Sorry!' Gertie says. Then she quickly ticks off the decorations and hurries away to do the next thing on her list.

Gertie checks on Markus. He is teaching
the little Moopers a welcome song.

'OK, mini Moopers.
Let's sing in our **loudest** voices!'

Some of the little Moopers are having a bit of trouble with the words. They begin to giggle.

Gertie starts **giggling** too!

'Gertie!' says Markus. 'Our guest arrives soon and we still haven't got the song right!'

Oh dear!

Gertie isn't taking this very seriously, is she?

In the banquet room, Mayor Beadle is **huffing** and **puffing** in the biggest fluster of them all. Lord Hoity Toity's visit is the most stressful time of year.

There are speeches to write,

buildings to inspect,

and a banquet to prepare.

Doesn't it look
delicious?

Moopertown's most famous chef is creating a **magnificent** dessert.

But right now
he is having a
lot of trouble.

Gertie bursts into
giggles.

'Gertie!' says the mayor. 'There is a time and place for giggling and the time and place is not now!'

Gertie sighs. 'I don't mean to giggle all the time,' she says. 'I can't help it if I find things funny.'

I hope she will do the right thing when their guest arrives, don't you?

Finally, the moment everyone has been waiting for.

This is very serious, Gertie tells herself.

I MUST NOT GIGGLE!

'Welcome, your Lordship!' says Mayor Beadle.
'We hope you will have a splendid time in our little town.'

Lord Hoity Toity

hurrumphs.

'We have prepared a magnificent banquet, and entertainment by Moopertown's finest performers.'

Lord Hoity Toity **hurrumphs.** again.

Hmmm. Lord Hoity Toity seems like a VERY SERIOUS person, doesn't he?

Gertie runs back to the Town Hall
to find the first performer.

Dom is pacing up and down.
'What's the matter?' Gertie asks.

'The fate of Moopertown rests on ME!'
Dom says dramatically. 'If I mess up my poem,
Lord Hoity Toity will have a terrible visit.
Oh, I need **more time** to practise!'

Gertie **pinches** her lips together.
'Don't worry. I'll ask the Moopertown
Choir to go first,' she says.

'Oh, would you?' Dom sighs. 'Thank you!'

Gertie rushes to the next room. The little Moopers are all dressed up and are **silly** with excitement.

'I can't go next!' Markus says.
'We need to practise one more time.'

Gertie swallows a giggle. 'Well, I guess I can
send little Looby with the welcome wreath.'

But when Gertie finds the tiny
Mooper, Looby is crying.

'I wost
my **toof!**' Looby says.

'She lost her tooth,' her mummy explains.
'Now she's worried she won't be able to say
Lord Hoity Toity's name properly. You know
how particular he is about his name!'

Gertie tries not to giggle. She puts on her
most serious face. 'I'll do the talking, Looby.
You just carry the wreath.'

Gertie and Looby enter the banquet room.

Lord Hoity Toity looks down his **very long**

nose at them and sniffs importantly.

'Please accept this gift from all of Moopertown!'
Gertie announces in her most serious voice.
'We welcome you, Lord Hoity —' she pauses.

'Lord Hoity Toity
Varon mon Burger ...?' she mumbles.

'Lord Hoity Toity
Moopen
bon
Vrooger?'

Oh no!
Gertie has forgotten
his name!

Gertie feels a bubble in her belly.
It fizzes and bounces about.
Finally, she can hold it back
no longer.

An enormous giggle bursts out.

Everyone gasps!

The more Gertie tries to stop her giggles,
the faster and louder they come.

Even though she is giggling, she feels terrible!

She has ruined
EVERYTHING!

But just then, Lord Hoity Toity's eyes begin to crinkle.

His mouth begins to twitch.

The Moopers see something they have

never seen before.

Lord Hoity Toity's mouth opens wide and a great
bellow of laughter **bursts out!**

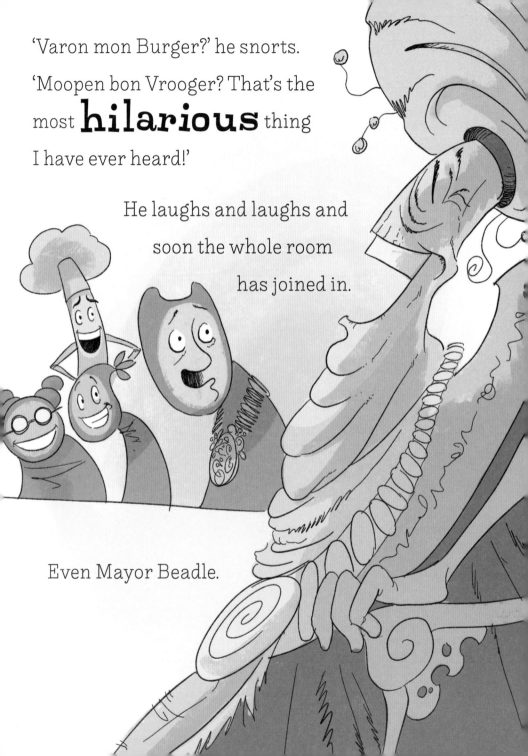

'Varon mon Burger?' he snorts.
'Moopen bon Vrooger? That's the
most **hilarious** thing
I have ever heard!'

He laughs and laughs and
soon the whole room
has joined in.

Even Mayor Beadle.

Lord Hoity Toity claps Gertie on the shoulder.
'I can't remember when I've laughed so hard!
Everyone is always so serious around me. But you
have reminded me how important it is to laugh.'

Oh Gertie, you truly are a ...

Gertie gasps in delight.

'Well then, I think it's time to **celebrate!'**
Mayor Beadle announces. 'Let the dancing begin!'

So the phoodle horn band plays, and the
Moopertown Choir joins in, and soon, everyone
has found someone to dance with.

Even little Looby.

All the residents of Moopertown sleep soundly
that night after a very long and exciting day.

Especially Lord Hoity Toity
Baron von Mooper.
(Who insists that from now on,
everyone just call him **George**.)